The Pony-Mad Princess

Princess Ellie's Secret

Diana Kimpton

Illustrated by Lizzie Finlay

USBORNE

For Jack

First published in 2004 by Usborne Publishing Ltd., Usborne House,
83-85 Saffron Hill, London EC1N 8RT, England. www.usborne.com

Based on an original concept by Anne Finnis.

Text copyright © 2004 by Diana Kimpton and Anne Finnis.
Illustrations copyright © 2004 by Lizzie Finlay.
The right of Diana Kimpton and Anne Finnis to be identified as the authors
of this work, and the right of Lizzie Finlay to be identified as the illustrator
of this work have been asserted by them in accordance with the Copyright,
Designs and Patents Act, 1988.

Cover photograph supplied by Sally Waters.

The name Usborne and the devices ♀ ⊕ are
Trade Marks of Usborne Publishing Ltd.

A CIP catalogue record for this book is available from the British Library.

JFM MJJASOND/09 89880

ISBN 9780746060193

Printed in Great Britain.

The Pony-Mad Princess

Princess Ellie's Secret

Ellie's heart sank. Deep down inside, she knew Miss Stringle was right. Shadow was her very first pony, and she could hardly remember the time when he wasn't there for her to love...what would happen to Shadow if she couldn't ride him any more?

Look out for more sparkly adventures of
The Pony-Mad Princess!

Chapter 1

"Steady, Shadow," said Princess Ellie.
The black Shetland pony she was riding
pawed at the ground with a tiny front hoof.
He was keen to start the dressing-up race,
and couldn't understand the delay.

"Are you all right down there?"
asked Kate, with a grin. She was riding
Sundance, Ellie's chestnut pony, who was

The Pony-Mad Princess

much taller than Shadow.

Ellie grinned back. "Just you wait," she said. "Sometimes it's good to be small." She was so glad Kate had come to live with her grandparents, who worked at the palace. It was good to have a friend at last, and they had so much fun together with Ellie's four ponies.

"Are you two ready?" called Meg, the palace groom. When they both nodded, she shouted, "One, two, three, GO."
The two ponies leaped forward and galloped across the field towards two piles of clothes on the other side. Ellie leaned forward, urging

Shadow on. But the Shetland's short legs were no match for Sundance. Soon, the chestnut pony pulled ahead and reached Kate's pile of clothes first.

"Bother," thought Ellie, as she saw Kate leap off and start putting on a long floppy coat. Then Shadow finally reached the other pile and she had to concentrate on her own part in the race.

Jumping off was easy – her feet were nearly touching the ground anyway. Then she pulled on a long coat, wrapped a scarf around her neck and crammed a wide-brimmed hat on top of her pink and gold crash cap.

The Pony-Mad Princess

She glanced over to Kate, expecting to see her on her way back. But she wasn't. She was struggling to mount Sundance. Now she was dressed up, she was finding it hard to lift her foot high enough to reach the stirrup.

"We've still got a chance, Shadow," cried Ellie. She didn't have Kate's problem. Shadow was so small that she managed to jump into the saddle without using the stirrups at all.

She urged the Shetland into a gallop and headed back towards the finishing line. Soon she could hear Sundance's hooves pounding after them, but this time the lead was too great. Shadow raced across the line just ahead of the chestnut pony.

"Ellie's the winner," shouted Meg.

"Well done," said Kate. "Being small was

definitely useful that time."

Suddenly a voice called, "Princess Aurelia!"

Ellie looked round and saw Miss Stringle standing at the palace end of the field. She always insisted on using Ellie's full name. To Ellie's annoyance, so did nearly everyone else in the royal household, especially the King and Queen. Ellie trotted Shadow across the field to say hello. But as soon as she was close enough to see her governess's face, she realized something was wrong.

"Whatever are you doing, Your Royal Highness?" asked Miss Stringle, giving Ellie one of her disapproving looks.

Ellie ignored the look and cheerfully replied, "We're playing mounted games. I just won. Did you see?"

"Indeed I did," declared Miss Stringle. "And I'm horrified to see you making such an exhibition of yourself. It is not suitable behaviour for a princess."

Ellie felt confused. Surely there was nothing wrong with winning. Then she remembered the hat, coat and scarf. "I had to wear these," she explained, as she pulled off the hat. "You can't have a dressing-up race without dressing up."

"I am not talking about the clothes," said Miss Stringle, crossly. "It's the pony that's the problem. It's much too small." As she spoke, she waved her hand at Shadow. The greedy Shetland instantly assumed he was being offered food. He stuck out his nose and nuzzled Miss Stringle's outstretched palm. She pulled her hand away quickly and dabbed it clean with a lace-trimmed hankie.

Normally, Ellie would have been tempted to laugh. But this time, she was too full of indignation. "Shadow's not too small," she said. "He's exactly the right size for a Shetland."

"But that's not the right size for *you*," said Miss Stringle. "You look ridiculous. I'll have to tell your parents." Without waiting for Ellie to reply, she marched back to the palace with a determined look on her face.

Ellie's heart sank. Deep down inside, she knew Miss Stringle was right. Shadow was her very first pony, and she could hardly remember the time when he wasn't there for her to love. He'd been her best birthday present the year she was four and he'd been just the right size for her then. But over the years, she had grown and he hadn't. Now her feet nearly touched the ground when she was riding him. She had hoped no one else would notice. What would happen to Shadow if she couldn't ride him any more?

Chapter 2

Ellie didn't have to wonder for very long. By the time she and Kate had ridden back to the stable yard, the King and Queen were already there. They looked strangely out of place in their royal clothes and everyday crowns. Their long velvet robes trimmed with ermine were definitely not designed with straw and manure in mind.

Miss Stringle was with them. She pointed at Ellie as she rode Shadow through the arched entrance. "You see what I mean, Your Majesty. The princess looks ridiculous."

The King stifled a laugh. "She's quite right, Aurelia. Shadow's much too small for you now."

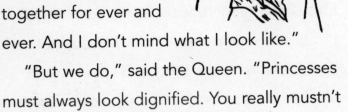

"But I love him," said Ellie. "We've been together for ever and ever. And I don't mind what I look like."

"But we do," said the Queen. "Princesses must always look dignified. You really mustn't ride him any more."

"Perhaps Kate could instead," suggested Ellie. "She's not a princess so you can't mind what she looks like." To Ellie's delight,

Kate agreed with enthusiasm. Perhaps this was the solution.

But the Queen smiled and shook her head. "That's a lovely idea, but Kate's legs are even longer than yours. And this isn't just about appearances. It's about what's right for Shadow."

"The fact of the matter is that you are both too big to ride him," said the King, firmly. Then he turned to Meg and added, "Please arrange for the pony to be sold."

Ellie was too shocked to speak. Not being able to ride Shadow was bad enough. Losing him would be unbearable.

Meg must have spotted her dismay.

"Don't worry," she said. "We'll find him a really good home."

Ellie jumped down and stood defensively between Shadow and the adults. "He doesn't need a good home," she said, angrily. "He's got a good home already." Shadow nuzzled in her pocket for a peppermint, unaware that his future hung in the balance.

The Queen put her arm round Ellie's shoulders. "I'm sure you'll get used to the idea, Aurelia."

16

Princess Ellie's Secret

"And you'll still have Sundance, Rainbow and Moonbeam," added the King. "Surely three ponies are enough for anyone."

Ellie watched miserably as her parents walked back to the palace with Miss Stringle. How could they be so mean? Didn't they understand how much she loved Shadow?

Sundance seemed to sense something was wrong. He reached out his chestnut head and blew gently down his nose at the Shetland. The two ponies had been friends ever since they first met. They often stayed together in their field, standing head to tail to protect each other from the flies.

Ellie stroked Sundance's chestnut nose. "You'll miss Shadow too, won't you?"

"So will I," said Kate, as she ran her fingers through the Shetland's black mane, then she glanced at Ellie and added, "It must be much harder for you."

Ellie flung her arms round Shadow's neck. "It won't feel like home without him. He's always been here. George taught me to ride on him."

Kate looked puzzled. "Was George the groom before Meg?" she asked. "The one who wouldn't let you help look after your ponies."

"Yes," said Ellie, as she gave the Shetland the peppermint he'd been looking for. She was so glad George had retired. Then she suddenly had an idea. "Hold these," she yelled, thrusting Shadow's reins into Kate's hands and racing after her parents.

They were already well ahead of her so she took a short cut, leaping over a low hedge and running across the neatly manicured lawn. They were just walking up the gravel path to the magnificent main entrance when Ellie squeezed between two large rose bushes and ran out in front of them. Miss Stringle's eyebrows shot skywards at the sight of such unprincesslike behaviour, but Ellie didn't have time to apologize.

"I've got a brilliant idea," she said. "We don't need to get rid of Shadow after all."

The King and Queen looked doubtful, so Ellie continued quickly before they could stop her. "He's worked really hard for years

19

just like George did. So couldn't he retire and be happy like George? Then it wouldn't matter that there's no one to ride him. He could just stay here and spend the rest of his life eating grass and doing nothing."

"Hmmm," said the King, thoughtfully. "I can't see anything wrong with that."

The Queen smiled. "It sounds like a perfect solution. You'd better go back and tell Meg." She glanced sideways at Miss Stringle and added, "But this time, use the path."

Ellie was so delighted that she gave her mum a big hug. Then she headed back to the stables, trying to walk in as dignified a way as possible until the royal party went inside. As soon as she was sure they couldn't see her any more, she started to run as fast as she could.

Princess Ellie's Secret

She found the others in the tack room and blurted out her news. Kate was as delighted as she was but, to Ellie's surprise, Meg seemed less enthusiastic.

"What's wrong?" Ellie asked her, angrily. "I thought you liked Shadow?"

Meg shook her head and smiled. "Of course I do. I'm just worried that retirement might not suit him as much as you think."

Ellie rushed away. She didn't want to hear Meg's doubts. She was sure her idea was brilliant. What could possibly go wrong?

Chapter 3

The next day, Ellie was in the middle of a dreary maths lesson when a footman arrived. Miss Stringle glowered at him. The schoolroom was her territory and she didn't like being interrupted.

The footman ignored the glower. He straightened the jacket of his red and gold uniform, pulled himself up to his full

height, and announced, "Their
Majesties, the King and Queen,
wish to see Princess Aurelia
immediately in the parlour."

Even Miss Stringle couldn't
ignore such an important
summons. She snapped her book
shut and waved Ellie towards
the door. "You'd better go,"
she said. "But make sure you
come straight back."

Ellie was delighted to escape, as she
loved going to the parlour. She was
fascinated by the dozens of animals
galloping across the painted ceiling, but
there was no time to look at those today.
The King and Queen were standing waiting
for her by one of the tall windows. Meg was

with them and so was the royal vet. They
all looked very serious.

Ellie's mouth went dry with fear.
Something must be terribly wrong. Had
there been an accident? Was one of her
ponies hurt or even dead?

"We've been talking about Shadow,"
said the King.

"Is he sick?" asked Ellie, her panic
growing worse by the minute.

"No," said the Queen. "But Meg is worried about him. She thinks retiring Shadow is a bad idea."

"No, it's not," argued Ellie. "He'll love doing nothing. He'll be able to stand in the field and eat all day long."

"That's the problem," said Meg. "Too much food and too little exercise will make Shadow very fat."

Ellie scowled at her. "What's wrong with that?" she snapped. She felt betrayed. Meg was usually on her side.

The King stepped between them. "Calm down, Aurelia," he said, firmly. "Being rude won't get you anywhere. We're only trying to do what's right for Shadow."

"It doesn't feel like it," Ellie muttered under her breath. She tried hard to look

25

calm although she didn't feel it inside.

The vet smiled kindly at her. "Shadow is a lovely pony," he said. "I can see why you're so fond of him."

Ellie felt a glimmer of hope and smiled back. Perhaps there was someone on her side after all.

The vet walked over to the fireplace and turned to face them, his hands behind his back. "The problem is that Shadow's a Shetland," he continued. "He's designed to work hard on poor grazing. If he does nothing but eat all day, he could get ill."

"With tummy ache?" asked Ellie, remembering the last time she'd eaten too much chocolate cake.

"No," said Meg. "With laminitis."

"What's that?" Ellie asked. She had seen the name in her pony books but she had never understood what it was.

"It's an illness that fat, over-fed ponies can get," explained the vet. "It makes the insides of their feet hot and inflamed. It's very painful and it can damage their feet so badly that they never get better."

"That's why I'm worried about Shadow," said Meg. "If he got laminitis, he'd really suffer."

The Queen walked forward and put a sympathetic arm around Ellie's shoulders. "So retirement isn't right for Shadow, is it, Aurelia?"

"No," said Ellie miserably, as the glimmer of hope disappeared. Her idea wasn't so brilliant after all. She'd feel dreadful if it made Shadow ill.

"I'm glad that's settled," announced the King. "Meg will arrange to sell him as soon as possible."

Ellie started to cry. "Please don't make him go," she begged.

"No amount of tears are going to make me change my mind," said the King. "Shadow needs plenty of exercise and the only place he's going to get it is in a new home."

Ellie knew she had lost. But she couldn't bear the thought of losing Shadow.

Chapter 4

Ellie found it hard to concentrate when she got back to the schoolroom. Her brain was too busy trying to think of a way to keep Shadow. Her thoughts were interrupted by Miss Stringle tapping her desk with a ruler. "So what is the answer, Your Highness?" she asked, impatiently.

"I'm not sure," muttered Ellie. That was

an understatement. She didn't even know what the question was.

"Think carefully," said Miss Stringle in an exasperated voice. "If there are twelve princesses and nine princes, how many couples can live happily ever after?"

"Twelve?" guessed Ellie.

Miss Stringle raised her eyebrows.

"Eleven?" said Ellie, watching the eyebrows closely. They didn't drop so she tried again. "Nine?"

"At last," said Miss Stringle with a sigh of relief. "Mental arithmetic is obviously not your strong point today. I think we'll try some history."

"Do I have to?" asked Ellie without enthusiasm.

"Of course you do," replied Miss

Stringle. "You're a princess. You must learn about your heritage." She pulled a huge book down from a shelf and laid it on Ellie's desk. "Maybe this will get you interested."

To her surprise, Ellie saw that it was an old photograph album. Its red leather cover was embossed with the royal coat of arms and a golden crown.

"Look inside," said Miss Stringle. "There are pictures of the entire royal family, starting from the days when photography was invented."

The Pony-Mad Princess

Ellie slowly turned the pages. This was much more interesting than learning the dates of ancient battles. "Look, she's wearing Mum's crown," she said, pointing at a photo of a long-dead queen.

"That's your great grandmother, Queen Elspeth," said Miss Stringle. "She had that crown made for her. She said the old one gave her a headache."

Ellie laughed and looked at the next photo. It showed the grumpiest-looking king she had ever seen.

Princess Ellie's Secret

"That's her husband – your great grandfather," explained Miss Stringle.

"He looks very cross," said Ellie. "Perhaps his crown gave him a headache too." She turned to the next page, where two small girls in frothy dresses and wide-brimmed hats smiled out at her.

"That's your grandmother and your Great Aunt Edwina when they were little girls,"

explained Miss Stringle. She pointed at the prim lady beside them. "And that's their governess. Doesn't she look elegant? Governesses were so respected in those days." She paused and sighed wistfully.

But Ellie wasn't listening any more. She didn't care who the people in the photo were. What was much more important was that they were sitting in a carriage, and that carriage was being pulled by a Shetland pony just like Shadow. Perhaps this was the answer to her problem. If Shadow learned to pull a carriage, it would keep him busy and give him plenty of exercise. Plus, she was sure that she and Kate would enjoy driving him around the palace grounds.

The more Ellie thought about the idea, the more she liked it. By lunchtime, she was convinced she had discovered the perfect solution to the Shadow problem. She was bursting to tell her parents the good news. But when she rushed into the dining room, she found them deep in conversation. They looked up briefly and smiled. Then they ignored her and went back to talking to each other.

Ellie considered butting in, but decided against it when she realized they were talking about taxes. Although she found that one of the most boring topics in the world, her parents seemed to find it fascinating. They definitely wouldn't like being interrupted, and she needed them in a good mood to listen to her plan.

She wandered across the room to choose what she wanted to eat from the silver dishes laid out on the sideboard. The selection of food was mouth-watering. There were cold meats and fish of every kind, tomatoes cut into lilies, delicate curls of cucumber and warm crusty rolls. Ellie was careful not to let the butler give her too much. She wanted to leave room for the profiteroles dripping in chocolate sauce, which were piled temptingly on a crystal dish.

She was just finishing the last of her smoked salmon, when the Queen finally stopped talking. She smiled at Ellie and asked, "Are you feeling better, dear? You looked so upset after our little talk."

Princess Ellie's Secret

Ellie smiled back. "I'm fine now," she said. "I've had..."

"Good," interrupted the King before Ellie could finish. "I'm glad you've realized that it's right to sell Shadow."

"No, no," cried Ellie. "We don't need to sell him. I've had the most wonderful idea."

"Not another one," sighed the King.

"This one's much better," said Ellie. "All we have to do is..."

"No," said the King, firmly. "We've made up our minds. We must do what's right for Shadow, and that means finding him a new home. The dealer is coming to collect him at the end of next week."

Ellie turned desperately to her mother for help. "Please listen," she begged. "This idea's perfect. I know it is."

But the Queen was just as firm. "I'm sorry, Aurelia, but it's already arranged. There is absolutely no point in arguing."

Ellie burst into tears and ran out of the room. She didn't even glance at the profiteroles piled uneaten on the sideboard.

But she wasn't going to give up. She was sure her idea would work. She just had to think of a way to prove it.

Chapter 5

Ellie was relieved when Kate came back from school. She needed to talk to someone who would listen – someone who would take her side and help her to keep Shadow.

They sat together in Ellie's bedroom while she told Kate the events of the day. It was the pinkest bedroom in the world. The King had designed it, and he was sure all princesses liked pink. Unfortunately, Ellie didn't.

Kate squealed with delight when she heard Ellie's idea about teaching Shadow to drive. "That's brilliant. It solves everything."

Ellie sighed. "It would if my mum and dad would let us do it."

"You'll just have to persuade them," said Kate.

"How can I?" groaned Ellie. "They won't even listen."

Kate sat on the rose pink carpet and looked at the pony posters which covered the pink and white striped wallpaper. "Maybe you should show them the photo," she suggested. "The one that gave you the idea in the first place."

Ellie brightened up. "I don't think they'd look at a picture. But what if we teach

Princess Ellie's Secret

Shadow to pull a carriage? Then we can show them the real thing and prove that my idea works!" She paused thoughtfully for a moment. "We'll have to do it in secret," she added. "We don't want them to stop us."

"That's brilliant," said Kate. "I love secrets. What do we have to do?"

"I'm not sure," said Ellie. "But we can soon find out." She grabbed her *Encyclopedia of Horses*, found the right page and started reading. But her excitement soon turned  to dismay. "It says here that it'll take at least six weeks to teach Shadow."

"That's hopeless," said Kate. "He'll be gone in less than two."

"I know," moaned Ellie. "There just isn't enough time."

They stared dismally at the book. Then Ellie suggested they went for a ride. "It'll cheer us up," she said. "And it might help us to think."

They fetched Moonbeam and Rainbow from the field, put them in their stables and went to fetch the grooming kit.

"Shut the door quickly," yelled Meg, as they stepped inside. A gust of wind had lifted the pile of papers she was reading and blown them all over the floor.

"Sorry," said Ellie, as she scrabbled about helping to pick them up.

"I'm looking for Shadow's paperwork," Meg

explained. Then she looked at Ellie's miserable face and added, "I'm sorry. I have to do what I'm told. And it is the best thing for Shadow."

Ellie stared angrily at the paper in her hand.

FINNISBARNE SHETLAND PONY STUD

BILL OF SALE

Supplied to HRH King Conrad
by the Finnisbarne
Shetland Pony Stud:
One six-year-old
Shetland pony.

Name: *Shadow of Finnisbarne*.
R and D.
Complete with tack.

"I think this is what you want!" she said, as she held it out to Meg. "What does 'R and D' mean?"

Meg looked at the paper with surprise.
"It's short for 'ride and drive'."

"And what does that mean?" asked Kate.

Meg smiled. "It means you can either
ride Shadow or you can harness him to a
carriage and drive him."

Ellie stared at her in disbelief. "So
Shadow knows how to pull a carriage?"

"Definitely," said Meg. "And all this time,
none of us knew."

"Wow!" cried Ellie with a triumphant grin.
"Maybe our plan will work after all."

Meg looked at her suspiciously. "What
are you two up to?" she asked.

Ellie hesitated. It was Meg who had
stopped her plan to retire Shadow. Would
she stop this one too?

Meg must have guessed what she was

thinking. "Don't worry," she said. "I won't tell anyone your secret unless it's going to put you or Shadow in danger."

"Thanks," said Ellie, and launched into an excited explanation of her idea and how there wasn't enough time to teach Shadow. "But he already knows how to pull a carriage so everything's all right," she finished in a rush.

"Remember he hasn't done it for ages," said Meg. "He'll need a quick revision course. And he'll need a set of driving harness the right size and something for him to pull."

"Could you ask your parents to buy them for you?" asked Kate.

"It's too risky," Ellie replied. "If I tell them our plan, they're sure to stop it."

Meg looked at the bill of sale again. "It says here that Shadow came complete with tack. I'm sure I've seen a set of harness around here somewhere. I wonder if it's his." She started burrowing through a pile of rugs in the far corner of the tack room. Ellie and Kate rushed to help in the search.

"There's so much stuff," said Kate, as she opened a cupboard and a pile of old stirrups tumbled out.

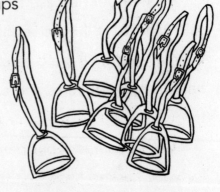

"I know," said Ellie, pushing a bundle of reins off a bench. "I don't think George liked throwing things away."

Suddenly, Ellie noticed that the bench

top had hinges. There must be a storage box underneath. She heaved open the lid and peered inside. To her delight, she found a set of black leather harness that looked just the right size for Shadow.

"That's solved one problem anyway," announced Kate.

"But we still need a carriage," sighed Ellie.

Meg took the harness from her and smiled. "Don't bother about that now. Go and have your ride. Moonbeam and Rainbow must be wondering what's happened to you."

The Pony-Mad Princess

The pleasure of riding soon pushed Ellie's worries about Shadow to the back of her mind. She and Kate rode up through the woods, exploring the twisting paths and jumping over fallen logs. When they reached the open hilltop, they had a long canter across the heather. Then they stopped to give the ponies a rest.

Kate looked down at the palace. "What are those buildings at the back?", she asked. "I've never noticed them before."

"They're just used for storing things," explained Ellie. "We hardly ever get rid of anything. Being royal means our old stuff isn't junk – it's history." Then she remembered the carriage in the photo. Was there a chance that it still existed?

Chapter 6

Ellie and Kate rode back to the palace as quickly as they could. They wanted to search the outbuildings right away, but there wasn't time before dinner. Luckily, the King and Queen had gone to a banquet in the town. That meant there was no long-winded formal meal for Ellie to sit through. Instead, she had supper with Miss Stringle and ate as quickly as she could without being accused of bad manners. As soon as she had finished, she pretended she had a headache and persuaded Miss Stringle to let her go to her room to watch TV. But instead, Ellie slipped outside to meet Kate, who was waiting at the kitchen door with a couple of torches.

"Are you sure it's a good idea to look now?" asked Kate, nervously. "It'll be dark soon."

Ellie felt nervous too, but she tried not to let it show. "We can't wait!" she said. "We're running out of time."

The outbuildings seemed bigger close up. They also looked dark and neglected. Ellie had never dared to go inside before.

Princess Ellie's Secret

There were sure to be spiders and maybe there were bats and rats as well. For a moment, her fear overwhelmed her and she wondered if they should abandon the whole idea. Then she thought of Shadow and knew she must keep going. She took a deep breath to calm herself and walked up to a large, wooden door.

"Won't it be locked?" said Kate. She sounded as if she'd be pleased if it were.

"Not necessarily," said Ellie. "They won't have put the crown jewels in here." She grabbed hold of the handle, turned it, and pulled.

The Pony-Mad Princess

The door creaked open unwillingly on rusty hinges.

The two girls crept inside. In the dim light from the grimy windows, they could see stacks of boxes, crates and strange-shaped objects shrouded with dustsheets.

"I don't think anyone's been in here for years," said Ellie.

"This stuff must be really old, then," said Kate, peering under the nearest dustsheet. The suit of armour underneath wobbled precariously and then crashed to the ground. The noise made both girls jump. It echoed around the building, sounding extra loud in the surrounding silence.

"Eeek!" shrieked Kate, when a mouse shot out of the helmet. It scuttled across the floor and disappeared.

Ellie ran in pursuit. "That's more the size of thing we're looking for."

"What? The mouse?" teased Kate.

"Don't be daft," said Ellie. "I mean this thing it's hiding behind."

She lifted the dustsheet and felt a thrill of excitement as she spotted a large wooden wheel. "Come on," she called, and wriggled underneath the sheet for a better look.

Kate followed her, and they both switched on their torches. But they didn't find a carriage. The wheel was attached to a strange, wooden hut.

"What on earth is it?" asked Kate.

53

"I think it's for getting changed in at the beach," said Ellie, who had seen something like it in a history book.

"I suppose your ancestors were too posh to wrap themselves in a towel like everyone else," laughed Kate.

She wanted to look inside but Ellie dragged her away. "We haven't got time," she said. "That's much too big for Shadow to pull. We've got to keep looking."

They searched and searched in the fading

light. But the only other thing they found with wheels was a strange-looking pram. Eventually, Kate looked at her watch by the light of her torch. "I'll have to go soon or my gran will get worried."

Ellie knew she'd have to go too. "Just five more minutes," she said, pointing to a pile of packing cases. "We haven't looked behind those yet."

They ran round the end of the pile and peered into the gloom. In front of them was something big, its shape hidden by a dustsheet. Ellie ran forward and peered under the edge. "There's a wheel," she yelled. Kate joined her and together they heaved the sheet onto the ground. Then they gave a whoop of delight. Standing before them was the pony carriage. It didn't look quite as smart as in the photo. The varnish was peeling in places and the cushions were filthy.

Kate lifted the shafts and tried to pull the carriage. Nothing happened. She pulled harder. Still nothing.

"Oh, no!" cried Ellie. "It must work." She grabbed hold of one of the shafts, leaving Kate with the other. "One, two, three, go," she yelled.

The two girls pulled as hard as they could. But it made no difference. The wheels were well and truly stuck.

Chapter 7

Ellie could hardly sleep that night for worrying. Kate had said her grandad would be able to make the carriage move. Ellie knew he was really good at fixing things, but suppose the wheels were stuck so firmly that even he couldn't shift them. What would they do then?

In the morning, she climbed out of bed feeling tired and gloomy. But she cheered up a little when she remembered it was Saturday and the start of half-term. Miss Stringle thought holidays were a waste of time, but Ellie didn't. What was the point in being a princess if she had to do lessons when all the other children in the kingdom were having fun? Since Kate's arrival at the palace, Ellie had insisted on having the same breaks as her friend. Now she was really glad that she had. With only a few days left to save Shadow, she couldn't afford to waste any time.

As soon as breakfast was over, she ran to her room and pulled on a pale pink fleece over her rose pink jeans. Then she tugged on her boots and raced downstairs towards the stables, wishing her father would buy her clothes that weren't pink. In the hall, she nearly collided with the King and Queen, who were walking along reading a letter. They looked very unhappy.

"What's wrong?" asked Ellie.

"It's Great Aunt Edwina," said the Queen with a sigh.

"Is she ill?" asked Ellie.

The King shook his head. "No," he said. "It's worse than that. She's fighting fit and coming to stay on Wednesday."

Great Aunt Edwina was an extremely difficult guest. Nothing was ever right and she constantly complained that everything had been so much better when she was a girl.

"It's a good thing you insisted on that holiday," said the Queen. "You'll be able to help us entertain her."

Ellie opened her mouth to say she was too busy. Then she shut it again quickly before any words came out. She couldn't risk giving away her secret now. But she needed every minute she could find to save Shadow. There was no time to spare for Great Aunt Edwina.

Kate was waiting for her in the stable yard, bubbling with excitement. "He's done it," she yelled.

"Who's done what?" asked Ellie.

"My grandad," replied Kate. "He's managed to move the carriage all the way to his workshop. It only needed some grease on the wheels to help them turn."

Ellie felt a twinge of disappointment that she hadn't been there to watch. But that was immediately swamped by her delight at the good news. Kate said her grandad was going to meet them later to show them how to make it as good as new.

In the meantime, they could concentrate all their efforts on Shadow. They brushed him carefully. Then they led him to the sand school where Meg showed them how to put on the harness.

"What are those?" asked Ellie, pointing to some pieces of leather beside Shadow's eyes.

"They're blinkers," explained Meg. "They stop him seeing the carriage behind him." She threaded the reins through some rings on a pad on Shadow's back and passed them to Ellie. "It's time to get started," she said.

"Don't we need these?" asked Kate, pointing at some straps Meg had left hanging on the fence.

"Not today," said Meg. "We won't need those until he starts to pull something."

Ellie stood behind Shadow wondering how to make him move. If she was riding him, she would squeeze him with her legs but she couldn't do that from the ground.

"Use your voice," said Meg.

"Walk on," called Ellie and, to her delight, Shadow immediately stepped forward, turning his ears towards her as he waited for the next instruction.

Ellie pulled gently on the reins and said

"Whoa" firmly. Shadow stopped.

"Brilliant," said Kate.

Ellie told Shadow to walk on again and they practised twisting and turning around the school. The Shetland behaved so well that Ellie became more ambitious. "Trot on," she called.

Shadow leaped forward eagerly into a bouncy trot while Ellie pounded along behind him. Shadow trotted faster and faster. Ellie struggled to keep up, but it was hard work running in the sand.

She was just about to tell him to walk again when she tripped and fell flat on her face.

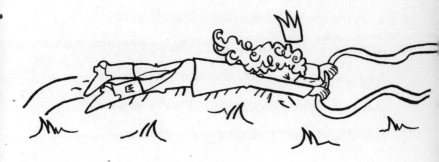

The Pony-Mad Princess

The fall knocked the wind out of her, but she kept hold of the reins. Shadow felt the pull on them and stopped. He turned his head round curiously to see what she was doing.

Meg ran over and took hold of his bridle, while Kate helped Ellie to her feet. "He coped with that brilliantly," Meg said. "But next time we'll practise where it's easier to run."

"Let's use the deer park," said Ellie, as she brushed the sand from her clothes. "You can't see it from the palace so no one will discover our secret before we're ready."

With that agreed, they set off to the workshop to start work on the carriage. Kate's grandad was already there. He patiently showed them how to rub down the peeling woodwork and paint on new varnish.

Princess Ellie's Secret

"You'll need to wear something old and tatty," he told Ellie. "That varnish will ruin those smart clothes of yours."

"But I don't have anything like that," she replied. "Princesses don't have tatty clothes."

So, for the next few days, Ellie worked on the carriage wearing a pair of Kate's grandad's overalls with the sleeves and legs rolled up.

Except for looking after her ponies, it was the nearest she had ever come to real work. Varnishing was a whole new experience and so was vacuuming the cushions.

In between their efforts on the carriage, the two girls continued with Shadow's lessons. The Shetland thrived on all the attention and soon progressed to happily pulling a log.

"He's doing really well," said Meg on Tuesday afternoon. "He's ready for his big test as soon as we can use the carriage."

"It looks fantastic now," said Ellie. "It's sure to be ready by tomorrow."

Unfortunately, Kate's grandad didn't agree. "Those wheels are still a bit stiff. I've got to do some more work on them and check the whole thing over to make sure it's safe. It'll be ready the day after tomorrow and not a minute earlier."

Princess Ellie's Secret

Ellie pleaded with him, but he wouldn't change his mind. So Shadow's first real drive was set for Thursday morning. Ellie knew that was cutting everything very fine. The dealer was collecting him on Friday. This would be his one and only chance to prove himself as a driving pony. It was vital that nothing went wrong.

Chapter 8

By Wednesday evening, Ellie was feeling really nervous. Suppose the carriage wasn't ready? Suppose Shadow hated pulling it? Suppose her parents were so angry with her that they insisted on selling him anyway?

She was forced to put her panic to one side when Great Aunt Edwina's ancient Rolls Royce roared up the palace drive. Ellie and

her parents waited to greet her at the main
entrance, while a nervous footman ran down
the steps to open the car door.

Great Aunt Edwina stepped out of the
Rolls, looking resplendent in a long skirt and
velvet cape. She glanced disapprovingly at
the footman. "Dear, dear," she said.
"Servants always looked so much smarter
when I was a girl."

"Here we go again," muttered the King
under his breath.

The Pony-Mad Princess

Ellie knew what he meant. She just hoped
that her great aunt's arrival wasn't going to
spoil her secret plan. There were already
enough things that could go wrong.

Luckily, the weather wasn't one of them.
Thursday morning was perfect for Shadow's
big day. The sky was blue, the birds were
singing, and sunlight glinted from the
distant sea.

Ellie put on her jeans and the only T-shirt
she had that wasn't pink. Then she headed
for the stables. But when she was only
halfway down the main corridor, she heard
the unmistakeable voice of Great Aunt
Edwina. "Aurelia, Aurelia," she called. Then
she glanced disapprovingly at Ellie's clothes
and added, "Oh my. Princesses never wore
trousers when I was a girl."

Princess Ellie's Secret

"They do now," said Ellie, as firmly as she could while still being polite.

"Your dear parents are a little busy this morning," said her great aunt. "They said they were sure you would be happy to keep me company."

Ellie smiled weakly. Her dear parents had obviously had enough of their difficult relative. Now it was her turn to suffer. Worse still, it meant there was no chance of her getting to the stables in time to get Shadow ready. She stopped a passing maid and sent her to the yard with a message saying she would meet the others in the deer park. Then she led Great Aunt Edwina to the largest of the palace sitting rooms while she desperately wondered how to get away.

"What shall we do?" asked her great aunt,

The Pony-Mad Princess

as she settled
herself in a red
velvet armchair.

Ellie ignored the "we" and
pulled a pack of cards from the
sideboard drawer. "You could play
patience," she suggested. Great
Aunt Edwina could play that by herself so
she wouldn't need Ellie's company.

"Nonsense," said the old lady. "We need
something we can do together. Fetch the
chess set."

Ellie sighed and did
as she was told. That
trick hadn't worked,
but she was
determined
not to give up.

Princess Ellie's Secret

She couldn't bear the thought of sitting inside all morning while the biggest event in Shadow's life was happening somewhere else.

It was hard to concentrate on chess with so many thoughts racing round her brain. Was the carriage ready? What was Shadow doing? Most important of all, how was she going to escape from Great Aunt Edwina?

Three games later, she still hadn't thought of a plan. She also wondered if anything ever made her great aunt happy.

"You've lost again, Aurelia," said Great Aunt Edwina, without seeming at all pleased to have won. "Maybe you don't practise enough. When I was a girl, your dear grandmamma and I used to play every day."

The mention of her grandmother made Ellie remember the two little girls smiling in the photograph. "I saw a picture of you both the other day," she said. "You must have been very young – only five or six, I think."

"It would be interesting to see that," said Great Aunt Edwina.

Ellie's eyes twinkled mischievously as she had an idea. "Come with me," she said. "I am sure my governess would be delighted to show you. She has masses of photos."

Ten minutes later, Ellie was on her way to the deer park, leaving Great Aunt Edwina talking about the good old days with Miss Stringle. Ellie glanced anxiously at her watch as she ran. She was very late. "I hope they haven't started without me," she thought. "And I *do* hope nothing else goes wrong."

Chapter 9

Ellie reached the deer park just in time. Kate was holding Shadow, while her grandad helped Meg to pull the carriage into position with one shaft on either side of the pony.

"It's great to see you," said Kate. "We thought you weren't going to make it."

"So did I for a while," said Ellie. "Great

Aunt Edwina nearly spoiled everything. She's a real nuisance." She helped lift the shafts through the leather loops called tugs on each side of the harness. Then she hooked one of the long leather traces to her side of the carriage, while Meg hooked on the other one.

"The traces are what he actually pulls the carriage with," explained Meg, as she adjusted the last few straps on the harness. "The shafts are only there to make him go straight."

Shadow had stood perfectly still while all this was going on, but now he stamped one tiny hoof impatiently on the ground.

"I think he wants to get started," said Meg. She climbed up into the carriage and took hold of the reins. "You two walk beside him for a while just to make sure everything is okay."

She told Shadow to walk on, and he moved forward willingly. Ellie was surprised how easily the carriage rolled after him. Kate's grandad had worked wonders on the wheels.

Shadow behaved perfectly as they practised stopping, starting, turning, and trotting. He even walked backwards a few steps when Meg told him to. Best of all, he seemed to be enjoying himself. He held his head proudly with his neck arched and his ears pricked.

Eventually, Meg stopped him and told Ellie and Kate to jump in the carriage. "He's a brilliant driving pony," she said. "There's no need for you to walk beside him any more."

Princess Ellie's Secret

The carriage swayed slightly as they climbed in. Ellie was surprised how different it felt from a car. The big wheels were designed to give a smooth ride, but it still bounced a bit as it rolled along.

As soon as Ellie was used to the feel of it, Meg swapped places with her so she could drive. Ellie felt very proud and slightly scared as she picked up the reins. Shadow was such a long way in front of her and there was no one to grab him if anything went wrong.

"You'll be fine," said Meg, reassuringly. "Just do what we've been practising all week."

Ellie's nerves rapidly disappeared once they set off. Soon, she was confident enough to ask Shadow to trot. It was a wonderful feeling bowling along in the carriage. There was no noisy engine like there would be in a car – just the sound of the wheels turning and Shadow's hooves pounding on the ground.

"Let's drive somewhere," suggested Kate. "It'd be more fun than just going round and round the same patch of grass."

The idea appealed to Ellie. She turned Shadow onto a gravel path lined with tall trees on either side. Their branches met high in the air, forming a tunnel of green. "We'll still be safe here," she said. "No one can see us from the palace."

Shadow's hooves crunched on the gravel as he carried them along. The sun glinted through the leaves making patches of light on the ground. It was a magical place – a place where almost anything could happen. Unfortunately, it did. When they rounded the next bend, they came face to face with Great Aunt Edwina.

Chapter 10

Ellie's heart sank as she pulled the Shetland to a halt. Trust Miss Stringle to mess things up. She must have persuaded Great Aunt Edwina to go for a walk.

"What are we going to do?" whispered Kate.

Ellie had no idea. She wanted to be the one to show Shadow's secret to her parents.

Princess Ellie's Secret

She didn't want her grumpy great aunt spoiling the surprise by moaning about it in advance. Then Ellie realized that, for the first time ever, Great Aunt Edwina was smiling.

"What a dear little pony," said the old lady, as she stroked Shadow's nose. He seemed to approve of the attention and nuzzled her long skirt searching for titbits. "He's just as sweet as the one I had when I was a girl."

Ellie was amazed. Great Aunt Edwina looked so different when she smiled. "Would you like a ride?" Ellie asked her. "There's plenty of room for four."

The old lady's smile grew even broader, and her eyes twinkled as she climbed into the carriage. "What I'd really like is to drive," she said. "I used to love driving when I was a girl."

Ellie shuffled closer to Meg to make room on the seat. Then she handed her great aunt the reins. The old lady took them expertly and soon had Shadow on the move again. At the end of the tree-lined path, Great Aunt Edwina turned him towards the palace.

"No!" shouted Ellie and Kate at the same time.

"Why ever not?" said Great Aunt Edwina. "I haven't had as much fun as this since I was a girl. I must show your parents."

Ellie tried to explain about the secret but there wasn't time. Before she had completely finished, they were driving up

Princess Ellie's Secret

to the royal garden where the King and
Queen were sitting in their outdoor thrones,
relaxing in the sun.

"Whatever's this?" said the King, jumping
to his feet in astonishment. The movement
dislodged his crown which slipped sideways
over one eye.

The Pony-Mad Princess

The Queen stood up in a more dignified manner. "Where did that carriage come from?" she asked. "And what's Shadow doing pulling it?"

The King looked at Ellie suspiciously. "Have you been up to something, Aur—?"

"Isn't it wonderful," interrupted Great Aunt Edwina. "I'm really enjoying myself."

The King and Queen stared at her in amazement. They had never seen their grumpy relative look happy.

"I'm so pleased," said the Queen.

"And so surprised," added the King in a very quiet voice as he pushed his crown straight.

Great Aunt Edwina winked at Ellie.

"I do hope I'll be able to do it again," she said, sweetly.

"So do I," said the Queen. "It's lovely to see you enjoying yourself so much."

Ellie leaped down from the carriage. "Does that mean we don't have to sell Shadow?"

The King looked doubtful. "I don't know. It's certainly exciting that Shadow can pull a carriage. But there's still the problem of his health."

"You don't have to worry about that any more," said Meg, helpfully. "Now we can drive him, he'll have plenty of exercise."

"So can he stay?" pleaded Ellie.

"Mmm," said her father, thoughtfully. Then he glanced at Great Aunt Edwina and smiled. "I don't know what you've been up to in secret, Aurelia, but it seems to have worked

87

out for the best. You can keep Shadow."

"And I should think so, too," said Great Aunt Edwina. "We never got rid of perfect driving ponies when I was a girl."

Ellie was so relieved that she nearly burst into tears. She threw her arms round Shadow's neck and hugged him. "You're safe now," she said. "You can stay here for ever and ever."

For more sparkly adventures of

The Pony-Mad Princess

look out for

A Puzzle for Princess Ellie

A Puzzle for Princess Ellie

Chapter 1

"Let's explore," said Princess Ellie, as she stopped Rainbow at the entrance to the wood. The path through it was like a long, dark tunnel. On one side was a high brick wall. On the other were trees growing so close together that their branches arched overhead and shut out the sun.

"Are you sure?" said her best friend, Kate. The palomino she was riding fidgeted from foot to foot, her golden coat gleaming in the sunshine. Moonbeam was the most nervous of Ellie's four ponies.

"Yes," said Ellie, firmly. She wasn't ready to go back to the palace yet. When she was there, she had to be Aurelia, not Ellie. She had to follow rules and behave like a proper princess. Out here she was free to do as she liked.

Ellie squeezed with her legs and Rainbow stepped forward obediently with her ears pricked. Kate followed close behind on Moonbeam.

"It's spooky in here," said Kate nervously, as they rode into the shade of the trees.

"Don't be silly," laughed Ellie. "Surely you don't believe in ghosts." Riding Rainbow gave her confidence. The grey pony was so brave and reliable.

It was very quiet in the wood. There were no birds singing and the path was covered with a thick, springy layer of rotting leaves that deadened the sound of the ponies' hooves.

As they rode deeper and deeper into the wood, Ellie looked round at the moss-covered wall and the damp tree trunks. "Kate's right," she thought. "It is a bit spooky in here." She pushed the grey pony into a trot, eager to reach the sunshine on the other side as quickly as possible.

Rainbow seemed uneasy too. She tucked in her head and blew down her nose nervously.

Suddenly, Rainbow stopped. Ellie was taken completely by surprise and shot forward out of the saddle. Rainbow didn't give Ellie time to recover her balance. Instead the grey pony whirled around on the spot, trying to head back the way they had come.

Ellie swung sideways. She felt herself falling and tried to grab hold of the saddle. But she had already gone too far. With a sickening thud, she landed flat on her back on the ground, clutching the reins tightly in one hand.

"Are you all right?" asked Kate, anxiously.

Ellie wasn't sure. She lay motionless for a moment, shocked by the force of her landing. Then she warily moved her arms and legs a little. To her relief, there was no pain. Nothing was broken. Only her pride was damaged. "I think so," Ellie finally replied, as she climbed slowly to her feet. She brushed the dirt from her pale pink jodhpurs and straightened the pink and gold silk cover on her hard hat.

Kate looked relieved. "I think Rainbow would be back at the stables by now if you hadn't kept hold of the reins."

"Steady, girl," soothed Ellie, as she walked up to the tense, uneasy pony and stroked her neck. "There's nothing to be scared of." Rainbow relaxed at the sound of her voice and rubbed her head gently on Ellie's shoulder.

"Shall we go back?" said Kate. "We don't want another accident."

"No," said Ellie. "I think she's all right now and all my books say you should never let a pony win." She put her foot in the stirrup and mounted quickly. As soon as Rainbow felt her weight in the saddle, she started edging back the way they had come.

"It's not time to go home yet," said Ellie, firmly. She turned the pony to face the spot where she had fallen off. This time she was ready for trouble.

To find out what happens next read

A Puzzle for Princess Ellie

The Pony-Mad Princess

Princess Ellie to the Rescue
ISBN: 9780746060186
Can Ellie save her beloved pony, Sundance, when he goes missing?

Princess Ellie's Secret
ISBN: 9780746060193
Ellie comes up with a secret plan to stop Shadow from being sold.

A Puzzle for Princess Ellie
ISBN: 9780746060209
Why won't Rainbow go down the spooky woodland path?

Princess Ellie's Starlight Adventure
ISBN: 9780746060216
Hoofprints appear on the palace lawn and Ellie has to find the culprit.

Princess Ellie's Moonlight Mystery
ISBN: 9780746060223
Ellie is enjoying pony camp, until she hears noises in the night.

A Surprise for Princess Ellie
ISBN: 9780746060230
Ellie sets off in search of adventure, but ends up with a big surprise.

Princess Ellie's Holiday Adventure
ISBN: 9780746067321
Ellie and Kate go to visit Prince John, and get lost in the snow!

Princess Ellie and the Palace Plot
ISBN: 9780746067338
Can Ellie's pony, Starlight, help her uncover the palace plot?

Princess Ellie's Christmas
ISBN: 9780746068335
Ellie's plan for the perfect Christmas present goes horribly wrong...

Princess Ellie Saves the Day
ISBN: 9780746068342
Can Ellie save the day when one of her ponies gets ill?

Princess Ellie's Summer Holiday
ISBN: 9780746073087
Wilfred the Wonder Dog is missing and it's up to Ellie to find him.

Princess Ellie's Secret Treasure Hunt
ISBN: 9780746085745
Will Ellie find the secret treasure buried in the palace grounds?